This book belongs to

....

The Mighty Adventures
of Flo & Mo

The World's Greatest Toy

Written by Amber Browne
Illustrated by Leana Ransom

There once was a girl and a very little boy, who decided to go on an adventure to find the world's greatest toy.

They travelled for weeks...
And weeks and weeks...
To lots of different countries,
and even mountain peaks.

They went to Australia and met a kangaroo, but when they asked him about toys, he didn't have a clue.

"Toys!" said Morris, loud and clear. So they jumped in a plane and Florence started to steer.

They flew through candy floss clouds and trees made of cheese. Swam through rivers full of slushie that led to the seas.

They saw a volcano erupt, spitting lava for miles and as they watched the excitement, they couldn't hide their smiles.

Still hunting for toys or teddies or dolls, they found themselves amongst a friendly bunch of trolls. They had a quick boogie whilst singing a song but then it was time to hurry along.

The next thing they saw they simply couldn't ignore.
ENORMOUS. HUMONGOUS.

Bigger than anything before!
A giant called Bertie carried them for part of their journey, whilst they had a quick drink as they were ever so thirsty.

So many wonderful things they
had seen, so many memories
to make their hearts beam.
But still they had not, found
one single toy, that even came
close to bringing such joy.

"Toys, toys, toys!" Morris shouted again. So they hopped in a boat this time, but soon got stuck in slime.

"Help!" yelled Florence, as loud as she could and just as she did there a unicorn stood...

They lept on her back as she began to shimmer, then she whooshed into the sky and filled it with glitter.

They slid down a rainbow all the way to the ground and you'll never believe it...
Can you guess what they found?

Yes! You guessed right, a big pot of gold.

But at the bottom of the money, they could see something funny.

A dinosaur! On roller skates!
Stuck to a spot in the middle of the pot.
"Would you like us to help you?" They both said
together. This really was becoming a
tremendous adventure.

So they helped Mr
Dino out of the pot
and the toys they
were looking for they
had almost forgot.

Before they could
think anymore about
toys, they were
distracted by
something.
Something making
lots of noise…

Crashing and banging whilst huffing and puffing, was a cute little dragon trying to fix up his wagon.

"Don't worry dragon" Florence said in a calm fashion. "If we all work together this won't take forever, we can fix it very quickly as it isn't that tricky".

A twist and a screw and the wagon was good as new.
"Phew" breathed Mr Dragon as he climbed up to drive.

"It's very nice to meet you, what are your names? I'm Clive!"

"My name is Flo and this is little Mo but we can't stay and chat as we really need to go. We've been searching all over for the world's greatest toy, but now little Morris is a very sleepy boy."

"Shall we go home now?" Mo yawned to Flo. "Yes little sleepy head, let's go home now. Let's snuggle under a cover" Florence said to her baby brother.

So back through the sand of the magical land, to the ship on the ocean with the poisonous potion...

Singing softly to the mermaids that showed them the way back, until their next BIG adventure after some sleep and maybe a snack.

The End.

Dedicated to my little inspirations…
My precious baby girl and my sweet-sweet boy. This
book is proof that you can achieve anything you put
your minds to!
You will both always have all of the love and support
you need to achieve whatever makes you happy in life.

xxx

Printed in Great Britain
by Amazon

41917887R00018